AF571731

Jargon 60

75 LIFE LINES

JAMES BROUGHTON

The Jargon Society · 1988

The Jargon Society wishes to thank the National Endowment for the Arts for support; and the following, who are among our recent patrons: Roy Neill Acuff, Carter Burden, Jo C. Tartt, Jr., Joella Bayer, Dr. Shelley M. Brown, Dan Gerber, Dewitt Hanes, Robert Mayville, and James Merrill.

Cover montage by Joel Singer
Frontispiece photo by Robert Pruzan

ISBN 0-912330-64-3 (regular edition)
ISBN 0-912330-65-1 (special edition)

Distributed by Inland Book Company
254 Bradley Street, East Haven CT 06512
Toll-free: (800) 243-0138

For Sally Foy Dixon

who asked me
what I had learned in my life

A TOAST

James Richard Broughton (aka 'Big Joy,' aka 'Sister Sermonetta,' aka 'The Modesto Catbird') will be 75 years old—by the silly way they measure time on this baleful earth—on 10 November 1988. What will the next, newly elected President of the United States of America make of this? An omelette made of angels' eggs, one hopes.

James's debt to Old Bill Blake is obvious. Less obvious is his fealty to Eubie Blake, for who rags the mirthless sancta of the Sober & Boring more wickedly and stylishly than JB?

Most poets over 40 become, in Kenneth Patchen's words, "beings so hideous that the air weeps blood." What to make of James, this man still full of felicity in his person and in his words? Another rare soul in this mature pantheon comes to mind: Franz Joseph Haydn, who remarked: "Since God has given me a cheerful heart, He will forgive me for serving Him cheerfully."

For each of his 75 years, we have asked JB for an aphorism. Is thy common talk just found aphorisms? asks Marlowe. Is not the Devil just God when He's drunk? asks Tom Waits. Whatever and whichever, *Life Lines* is a monument to that vestigial art known as Wisdom, despite the fact that in the Land of Yup, we're in a place "where ignorance is bliss" and where " 'tis folly to be wise." This snazzy opusculum is both a guide for the young and balm for the aged.

To give James one to grow on as he approaches this zany birthday, allow me to quote something he said way back when: "In school time learn, in love time sing, in wisdom ripen. Allness is ripe." As we'd say here in the Cumbrian Dales: Long life, lead in your pencil, and mud in your eye, you daft old booger! Cheers!

JONATHAN WILLIAMS
Corn Close,
Dentdale, Sedbergh,
Cumbria

Everything is perfect as it is
except for the things that haven't yet got it right.

Nothing is new. Everything is renewal.
Life's major challenge: getting reborn often enough.

Since we are formed of cosmological dust
let's clasp one another and kick up a storm.
Only to the enraptured does the prophetic speak.

If you feel completely at a loss
you are probably on the right track.

Since nobody knows the meaning of existence,
the limits of the universe, or the cure for a cold,
we are free to delight in the mysteries of ignorance.

Innocence is the holiness of sagacity.

Believe the unbelievable. Enliven the unlikely.
Always carry change for the unchangeable.

What distinguishes one human from another:
the capacity to love and the ability to wonder.

Wonder is my pleasure, love is my elation,
friendship is my hobby, rapture my vocation.

People live in their wrongheads,
not in their right minds.

Most minds oscillate between sense and nonsense.
The rest don't oscillate at all.

People who take a dim view of life
dwell in a murky doldrum.
The easiest thing to find is fault.

Many nobodies who have studied nothing
are busy teaching it to everybody else.

Everyone needs a hole in the head
to let out the pollution.
The lowest common denominator sinks lower every day.

A dull prospect befogs the road to derring-do.
Exchange your mind for one with a better view.

Men are windowless monads
waiting for someone to raise their blinds.

People don't grow up. They just get taller.
People don't change. They just get more so.
Adults are deteriorated babies.

I love all men, except for those I can't stand.

When there's nothing you can do about anything,
do everything you can.

Muster the agile and compassionate.
Educate a humanity that will not embarass the earth.

Stand firmly, sit serenely,
mutter profoundly, sing recklessly,
dance all the way to your death.

You are capable of extraordinary actions:
you can pee, sneeze, fart, puke, snore, shiver.
Are you sufficiently amazed by your mechanisms?

Your soul goes out to the ends of your toes.
Go out with it!
It walks around everywhere on two legs.

We contain as much as we can imagine.
When we dance we jiggle the stars.

Make your home in left field. There's more room there.
Everybody wants to be in the right.

Never disown your mad superstitions,
bad habits, unclad fantasies.
Those are the riches of your personality.

Three cheers for agony, muddle and euphoria.
Without them there would be nothing to read.

The greatest enemies of the public good
are education, religion and law.
What's good for the public it never gets:
riotous living and peace of mind.

The heavyhanded and the leadfooted
keep crowding one off the dance floor.

Dreary food is the main cause of social unrest.
Winedrinkers know the merriment of the blessed.

Governments are a conspiracy of the mad and the inane.
Pass laws for the abolition of laws!

Don't fall asleep at the wheel of fortune.
Don't exercise, dance. Don't diet, chuckle.
Don't tell people what not to do.

Crazy old men are essential to society.
Otherwise young men have no suitable models.

Be fond, not wary.
Fear of love is fear of the sublime.

Every penis is on the firing squad of creation.
Every penis wants to belong to a new Adam.

Never resist any temptation. Except celibacy.

Be generous with joy and juicy with ripening.
Amplitude is the shape of splendor.

Enrich your repertoire of useless acts.
Watch waterfalls, sniff lilacs,
reply to meadowlarks, attack artichokes.

It is harder to love the world than to denounce it,
harder to embrace existence than to renounce it.

Reality isn't made of concrete. It's a seminal soup.
Savor it, swim in it, season it with piss and vinegar.

Your instincts are mythical heroes
eager to launch impossible adventures.

Do not die without learning what you can accomplish.
Fervor is eager to explode in all your molecules.

Misery is not an ultimate truth.
Authentic wisdom is a laughing matter.

Happiness takes a risk, misery plays it safe.

Wisdom is the least popular goal of humanity.
To be wise one must be foolish, foolhardy and foolproof.

Overthrow the tyranny of the humorless.
Commit the dead serious to funeral homes.
Trust only what opens, what reveals, what lights up.

Everything that is, is Light.
Except on very dark days.

Make florid mistakes. Laugh more and wash less.
Eat more chocolate than beans. Fuck often.

Desires are not bushes to be pruned.
A man is not meant to be a bonsai.

Life's essentials:
champagne, furry slippers, foreplay.

Buddha was a nil-boy killjoy.
Life is not a suffering duty.
Desire awakes the sleeps of beauty.

Cultivate your own form of workaday lunacy.
Otherwise you can't feel at home in the world.

If you soften your brain, it won't get brittle.
Add nuts when you go bananas.

When you have to fight fire with fire,
go jump in the lake.

Open your jocular vein! Spurt jocosity!
Laughter like garlic is a flavorsome cure-all.

Offend the righteous: ramble, dawdle, dabble.
And picnic in the cemetery.

Introduce your heart to the practice of hilarity
or the Good Life will prove a lifelong rarity.

Sexual orgies are less harmful to society
than political parties.

More and more profligacy!
How else shall we all connect?
One good fuck is worth a hundred debates.

Sexuality is the sport of the gods.
Eternity is in love with orgasm.

We fall in love in order to experience
bodily upheaval and spermatic visions.
This causes us to shudder and sweat,
exude gummy verbiage and sprout wings.

Love should unite mankind,
not split it up into exclusive couples.

Two things for lovers are a must:
equality of soul and mutual lust.

Hook up some chariots of chum.
We are already late for the camerado races.

Ride a saddle of unbridled spirit
and follow the trails that do not yet exist.

Leave pigeonholes to pigeon droppings.

Change everything, except what you love.
Love everything that changes your mind.

To keep from feeling degraded by the times
bathe in a brook, sleep in a barnyard,
hula in the office, somersault in church.

Come live with me and be my life
and we shall have no need of wife.

Reaching what you can is not enough.
Reach what you cannot!

Strengthen lofty connections.
Muses and angels want to be called on,
gods appreciate a pat on the back.

God is man's largest diversion.
And man is God's favorite toy.

Recipe for the creative life: remove safety belts,
plug loopholes, burn down safe retreats,
get reborn often, compose like a frolicsome child,
and never ask the end.

Serve forth your ripeness before it rots.

Live Love Laugh Leap
Sing Swim Sink Sleep

THIS edition was designed and produced by the Arion Press in San Francisco, with 75 copies bound in boards and 1500 copies in wrappers. The types are Bodoni Semi-bold, Bold and Ultra.